10.89

P9-BYJ-049

10.89

F
SMI

Smith, Janice Lee.

It's not easy being
George : stories
about Adam Joshua
(and his dog).

It's Not Easy Being George

It's Not Easy Being George

Stories About Adam Joshua (And His Dog)

BY JANICE LEE SMITH
drawings by Dick Gackenbach

Harper & Row, Publishers

IT'S NOT EASY BEING GEORGE: STORIES ABOUT ADAM JOSHUA (AND HIS DOG)

Text copyright © 1989 by Janice Lee Smith
Illustrations copyright © 1989 by Dick Gackenbach
Printed in the U.S.A. All rights reserved.

1 2 3 4 5 6 7 8 9 10

First Edition

Library of Congress Cataloging-in-Publication Data
Smith, Janice Lee, 1949-
  It's not easy being George : stories about Adam Joshua (and his dog)
by Janice Lee Smith ; drawings by Dick Gackenbach.
      p.   cm.
  Summary: More zany episodes in the life of Adam Joshua, as he
shares problems with his "ordinary" dog George and lives through
such school events as a pet show and an all-night sleepover in the library.
  ISBN 0-06-025852-7 : $. — ISBN 0-06-025853-5 (lib. bdg.) :
$
  [1. Dogs—Fiction. 2. Schools—Fiction. 3. Humorous stories.]
I. Gackenbach, Dick, ill. II. Title.
PZ7.S6499It 1989   88-33075
[Fic]—dc19   CIP
                                                              AC

Dedication

When I began the first Adam Joshua story, I was joined at the typewriter by a friendly five-year-old. He was full of enthusiasms, misgivings, and numerous strong opinions, which he refused to keep to himself.

He adored Superman, books about Superman, best friends who liked Superman, and pepperoni pizza. He wavered on the subjects of baby sisters, baby-sitters, monsters of any size, and school.

Delighted and humbled, I tried over the years to capture a portion of that spirit, complexity, and joy, to create the character of Adam Joshua. While I was about it, the small boy grew into a confident young man.

Eighteen this year, he's ready to move into a bigger world and handle a few monsters on his own. He's still full of strong opinions and a high zest for living. Young women and old cars have taken the place of most other interests (certainly school, and maybe even Superman!). And although he's more fascinating than ever, he won't let me take notes about him anymore.

This is a thank you to him. Life with you has been a celebration, Bryan. We're going to miss you so.

Contents

It's Not Easy Being George

Pet Day

One of the things Adam Joshua liked best about school was his teacher, Ms. D.

One of the things he liked best about Ms. D. was that she had good ideas.

One of the best she'd ever had was Pet Day.

"You're just going to love it," Adam Joshua told his dog, George, as they cuddled down together in bed at night.

George yawned.

"Ms. D. says that on Pet Day everybody in our class gets to bring their pets for everybody else to see. Nelson is bringing his fish, and

1

Angie is bringing her hamster, and Sidney is bringing Fleabitten, his cat."

George looked a little more interested.

"Ms. D. says that we can have Pet Day outside because it's been warm enough, and that way we can spread out a lot and then all the pets won't fight."

George looked very relieved.

"Ms. D. says we're going to have to work hard to get organized," Adam Joshua said. "But don't worry. I'll do all the organizing, and you can just come as the guest."

George fell asleep.

Adam Joshua could tell George was so excited he could hardly wait.

"My fish are very excited, Adam Joshua," his best friend, Nelson, said as they walked to school together the next morning. "Except for Cleopatra. You know how shy she is."

Adam Joshua nodded. Cleopatra swam away every time he tried to look her in the eye.

"I told my fish I don't think any other fish

are going to be there," Nelson said, looking a little worried. "I haven't heard about any other fish, have you, Adam Joshua?"

Adam Joshua shook his head.

"That's good," Nelson said, looking relieved. "You know how jealous my goldfish, Long John, can get."

———

When they got to their classroom, everyone was talking at once trying to tell everyone else about their pets.

Elliot Banks was talking the loudest.

"My dog, Champion, is a spitz," he said, getting even louder when he saw Adam Joshua.

Adam Joshua hadn't known there were any other dogs coming.

He sighed. If there did have to be another dog coming, why did it have to be one that belonged to Elliot Banks?

"Spitzes can do all kinds of tricks and are very clever," Elliot said, smirking at Adam Joshua.

Adam Joshua had worked hard for a long

time trying to teach George tricks. George had worked hard for a long time not learning them.

"I don't have a pet yet," Ralph said, "but I'm going to get one for this. I told my parents that Ms. D. said I had to have one. I said it was homework."

"My best fish for tricks is Felix," Nelson said. "I've nearly taught him to swim in a loop."

"My dog, Champion, can roll over and play dead and walk on his hind feet," Elliot interrupted.

"Julius is sort of the boss fish," Nelson said. "He says what he thinks and most of the other fish usually agree with him."

"Spitzes are tough and strong and make great guard dogs," Elliot said.

Adam Joshua pretended he wasn't listening, and if he was listening, that he wasn't impressed. Tough wasn't exactly what you'd think of when you looked at George.

Ms. D. came into the room and started shooing everyone to their desks.

"The judges are going to love Champion,"

Elliot whispered with a chuckle as he sauntered by.

Adam Joshua had forgotten there were
going to be judges.

He didn't think he'd tell George.

———

"I know you're excited," Ms. D. said, laughing. "But we've got to get a lot of regular work
done today so we'll have the time we need for
Pet Day."

Sidney raised his hand.

"My cat, Fleabitten, hates birds," he said,
"so we'll have to keep him away from birds."

"That's part of getting organized," Ms. D.
said, "and we'll have to get all those things
figured out. Remember, I want each of you
to learn as much as you can about your pet
so you can answer lots of questions. That way,
anyone who might want to get a pet like yours,
or who is just interested in it, can find out all
about it."

Sidney raised his hand.

"My cat hates hamsters too, so he can't be
around hamsters."

"We'll keep that in mind," said Ms. D., handing out math papers.

"My cat's not too crazy about people either," said Sidney.

———

Adam Joshua walked down the hall and went into the rest room and looked up in the corner of the ceiling for Alice.

"I don't know if you've heard," Adam Joshua told Alice, "but we're going to have a Pet Day." Alice didn't say anything, but Adam Joshua didn't worry about it. Alice was always pretty quiet, even for a spider.

"I'm going to bring George, and I'll make sure I bring him in to meet you," Adam Joshua said. Alice nodded.

———

"Time to get organized," Ms. D. said after they had done math and science and all the other things Ms. D. loved them to do.

Everybody made a sign to put up by their pet.

"I'll take a piece of poster board too," Ralph said, "even though I don't have my pet yet. I told my parents I had to get a pet, and they said they'd think about it." Ralph took two pieces of poster board. "They might think big," he said.

"Tell us a lot about your pet on the sign," Ms. D. said, "and I'll be around to help you on spelling."

"Fleabitten—A Really Rotten Mean Cat," wrote Sidney.

"George—My Dog" wrote Adam Joshua.

"Champion—A Champion Spitz," wrote Elliot. "He's also the most beautiful dog in the world," he said, drawing a dog on the poster. "He has fluffy white fur, and pointed ears, and a tail that curls perfectly."

Adam Joshua drew a picture of George, with his stomach dragging on the ground.

"Reba—An Exotic Snake," wrote Martha, drawing a swirl of brown and yellow across her poster. She added two eyes and a tongue sticking out at one end of it.

Adam Joshua drew George's ears hanging down in his eyes.

Nelson used three posters just to write the names of his fish.

"Cleopatra, Long John, Felix, Jonah, Ziggy,

Igor," he said, muttering while he was writing.

Elliot started drawing trophies and blue ribbons all around the edges of his poster.

Adam Joshua drew George's tail looking a bit ragged, because his baby sister, Amanda Jane, was always chewing on it.

"Adam Joshua," Ms. D. said, going by and stopping to look at Adam Joshua's sign, "don't you know what kind of a dog George is?"

Adam Joshua had once spent a lot of time trying to find that out. He didn't have the faintest idea what kind of a dog George was. He didn't think George had the faintest idea either.

"He's just George," he told Ms. D.

"Good enough," Ms. D. said, moving along.

"Jaws—A Guppy," Nelson muttered, still writing.

———

After Adam Joshua got home from school, he got out sticks, and balls, and an old sock George liked to chew. George was in the kitchen under Amanda Jane's chair, eating raisins as she threw them down to him. Adam Joshua picked up George and kissed Amanda Jane.

"Don't feel bad," he told her. "Probably after Pet Day we'll have a day for sisters. First things first," he said.

He carried George into the backyard and put him down in the middle of it where George couldn't find too many other things to do.

"Fetch!" Adam Joshua yelled, throwing the stick for George.

George sat there.

"Fetch!" Adam Joshua yelled, throwing the ball.

George got interested in a bird flying by, and watched it with his head tilted back.

"Fetch!" Adam Joshua yelled, throwing the sock.

George stopped watching the bird and started howling at a squirrel in a tree.

"I don't want to worry you," Adam Joshua told George, dropping down to sit on the grass beside him, "but Elliot's dog, Champion, is the

9

kind of dog that does tricks. I've told you all about Elliot. Champion is just the kind of dog he'd have."

George didn't look too worried.

"A lot of tricks," Adam Joshua said.

George looked a little more worried.

"Champion is the kind of dog that wins ribbons and prizes, and is very smart. His ears don't even droop," Adam Joshua told George.

George looked awful.

Adam Joshua thought it was about time.

———

At school they made a map of where each pet would go so there wouldn't be fights.

"Write down the animals your pet might have a problem with," Ms. D. said, "and we'll make sure to put them in the best place."

"I don't know what I'm getting yet," Ralph said, raising his hand. "It'll probably be a dog and it'll probably be big. Can I let you know later?"

"That will be fine, Ralph," said Ms. D.

"I think you'd better put my cat, Fleabitten, in a corner by himself," Sidney said, raising his hand too. "He just hates everything."

"Not near Sidney's cat, anybody's dog, babies, or anything else that crawls into fishbowls," Nelson muttered as he wrote.

Adam Joshua thought about George. George liked everybody. He never growled at cats, or chased birds, or bit at anything. He always tried to crawl into Nelson's fishbowl, but Adam Joshua thought that was because he wanted to get to know Nelson's fish better.

"Can go anywhere," Adam Joshua wrote. He thought about it a minute. "Not next to Angie's hamsters," he added.

Angie's hamsters were always sick, or nearly dying, or totally dead. Adam Joshua didn't want to hurt Angie's feelings, but he didn't want George catching anything either.

"And not near Angie's hamsters," Nelson muttered, finishing up.

"I think we'll put some of the delicate animals in the classroom," Ms. D. said, "rather than outside. If you think that's a good idea for your pet, please make a note of it."

Nelson opened his desk and rummaged until he found a pen.

"Very Delicate," he wrote across the top of his paper.

He underlined it twice.

———

"I'll see you tomorrow!" Ralph said as they hurried out the door after school. "I'll bet I have a dog by tomorrow, Adam Joshua. A big dog. I'm going to name him Bruno, and I'll be sure to bring him over to meet George!"

"Don't you plan on bringing that snake anywhere near me," Heidi told Martha as they headed off down their sidewalk.

"I hope my hamster stays alive for tomorrow," Angie said, waving good-bye.

"Everyone's very excited that my fish are coming, Adam Joshua," Nelson said as they walked. "Even Ms. D. says she can't wait to meet them."

Most of the time Adam Joshua couldn't stand Nelson's fish, but he knew Ms. D. was the type that liked everybody.

"Julius has been so nervous he's been having trouble sleeping at night," Nelson said. "He just keeps swimming in circles."

Nelson waved good-bye as he started toward his own house.

"Of course, it's a round bowl," he called back.

———

When Adam Joshua got home, George came running out to meet him like he always did, and licked him all over like he always did, and sat on the bed to listen while Adam Joshua told him about his day.

"We're all ready," Adam Joshua told George, "and except for Elliot and Champion, I think you're going to love it."

Out his bedroom window, Adam Joshua could see into Nelson's bedroom. Nelson was busy cleaning out his fishbowl and singing to his fish.

Other people, mostly Elliot, were probably washing and brushing and curling their dogs right now.

The last time Adam Joshua had tried to give George a bath, the bathroom had ended up soaked, and Adam Joshua had ended up soaked, and Amanda Jane had tried to help and fallen in with her clothes on. Adam

Joshua's mother had ended up furious, and George had ended up still dirty.

George looked pretty dusty for Pet Day, but Adam Joshua didn't think he'd try another bath.

"This is your last chance," Adam Joshua told George politely. "Are there any special tricks you'd like to learn?"

George hopped off the bed and headed out the door.

"That's what I thought you'd say," Adam Joshua yelled after him.

———

Late that night, after Nelson's bedroom was dark, and George was asleep, Adam Joshua stayed awake and worried.

It was nice to know Nelson's fish, Julius, was doing the same.

Adam Joshua worried that George was going to feel just terrible when he saw Champion.

He worried that George was going to feel really dumb.

He worried that other people were going to think George was dumb too.

15

He worried that he might start thinking George was dumb himself.

"But you're not dumb," he whispered to George, "you're just smart in ways people can't see."

George snored.

George always listened to everything Adam Joshua told him about school, and he agreed with everything Adam Joshua told him about things like Superman, and he laughed at Adam Joshua's jokes. He watched over Amanda Jane when Adam Joshua wasn't there to do it.

Adam Joshua had never taught George those things. Somehow George just knew.

Whenever Adam Joshua felt awful, George was always right there to try to cheer him up.

Maybe George wasn't much of a dog, but he was the best friend Adam Joshua ever had.

"So don't worry about Champion," Adam Joshua whispered. "You're going to do just fine."

George opened one eye and glared at Adam Joshua.

"Right," Adam Joshua whispered, shutting up and going to sleep too.

———

"You're going to be wonderful," Adam Joshua told George the next morning.

He pushed George's ears out of his eyes, and his chin and cheeks up to make him smile.

He used his father's toothbrush to brush George's teeth, brushed some dust off him, and fluffed his ears up so the droop wasn't so droopy.

"We're ready," said Nelson, standing at Adam Joshua's back door. He had a fishbowl in his hands and a book about fish tucked under his arm, and he was wearing a tag that said, "FISH EXPERT—JUST ASK ALL THE QUESTIONS YOU WANT."

George went crazy the minute he saw Nelson's fish.

"We can't walk together, Adam Joshua," Nelson hollered, standing on his tiptoes with the fishbowl high above his head. "You wait until I get to the end of the block, and then you can follow."

17

Adam Joshua and George walked a block behind Nelson and his fish all the way to school. George jumped and howled and tried to run, and Adam Joshua held on to tree trunks to stop George, and dug his heels in to slow him down, and sat on him when he had to.

"Adam Joshua," Nelson yelled back when they were almost there, "this wasn't such a good idea either. Julius says this whole thing is making him very nervous."

When Adam Joshua and George got to the school, there were pets everywhere.

A pet mouse peeked out of Heidi's pocket. Nate carefully carried a box of worms.

Martha wore her snake, Reba, wrapped twice around her shoulders.

Sidney was dragging his cat, Fleabitten, on the end of a leash. It was hissing and snarling at Sidney and everybody else.

Lizzie was dragging an empty leash, but she talked to it all the while anyway.

"This is Tansy," Hanah said as she scurried up pushing a baby carriage. Adam Joshua

19

looked in the carriage. A white cat popped its head up from under a blanket. It had a pink bonnet on its head, tied with a ribbon under its chin. It wore a blue sweater.

"She's very happy to meet you," Hanah said, pushing Tansy's head back under the blanket again.

Angie carried a cage.

"This is Walton Eight," she said, stopping beside Adam Joshua, "my new hamster. Number seven kicked the bucket last Friday."

Adam Joshua looked closely at Walton Eight. He was skinny and scrawny and had a bow around his neck.

"I sort of fluffed him up for Pet Day," Angie said. "It's about the best he ever looks."

"This is where we're going to be today," Adam Joshua told George, showing him a table with the sign "GEORGE" sitting on it. He fastened the leash to the table leg.

"You stay right here," he said, "and I'm going to check on Nelson, and then I'll be right back."

Nelson was standing at the door of the class-a thing. So then my mother tried, and now that stupid bird only says what she tells him to say."

"This room is a disgrace," said Sebastian.

George lay down beside the table leg and got quiet. When Elliot got to the table across the way with his dog, Champion, George didn't even bat an eye.

"So that's your great dog," Elliot said, shaking his head. "This is going to make you feel terrible," he laughed. "Just watch."

Elliot threw a stick and Champion fetched it. Elliot said, "Roll Over!" and Champion rolled over. Elliot said, "Play Dead!" and Champion did.

"Let's see what your dog does, Adam Joshua," Elliot said, chuckling.

Adam Joshua looked at George. George curled up a little tighter and closed his eyes, and pulled his ears down over them.

"Later," said Adam Joshua. "He wants to rest right now."

"That's too bad, Adam Joshua," Elliot grinned, getting out a special brush to fluff

room. "I don't believe it," he whispered, looking awful.

Tyler was already there, taking up the center of the room. Beside him was a big aquarium full of more types of fish than Adam Joshua had known existed. There were yellow and purple and blue ones and, zipping around up in the corner, a plump red one.

Nelson didn't say anything. He took his bowl of fish over to a table in the corner, and then he stood looking at them a minute and moved the bowl to a table under the window where they could have more light. He took a big breath and looked at Adam Joshua.

"You have very nice fish, Tyler," Nelson said.

Tyler looked surprised.

"Yeah, I guess so," he said. "My parents keep buying them for me, and I guess they can be pretty interesting."

"What are their names?" Nelson asked, moving closer to the aquarium to get a better look.

"I never thought about giving them names,"

Tyler said, shrugging. "I can't even tell a of them apart."

Nelson looked a little sick, and went to sta by his fish at the window again.

He patted the bowl.

———

When Adam Joshua got back outside, th was a parrot on the table beside Geo George had his paws up on the table and nose against the parrot's cage, trying to friendly.

"Pick up your dirty socks," said the pa He reached through the cage and bit Ge on the nose.

"Sorry," Jonesy said as George dove u the table. "This is Sebastian and he's no nicest bird. In fact," said Jonesy, "I don't like him much."

Adam Joshua crawled under the tabl pulled out George.

"Don't talk to strangers," he said, k George where Sebastian had bitten him

"Besides," Jonesy said, "for a month to teach Sebastian to talk, and he would

23

up Champion's fur. "My dog just never seems to get tired."

———

Ralph shuffled up slowly with a small glass aquarium. He put it on a table close to George.

"It's a lizard," he said, sighing. "It turned out that my dad is allergic to a lot of animals, and my mother can't stand a lot of animals, and she said a whole lot of other animals were just too much work. After a while, a lizard was all that was left. I named him Bruno anyway." Ralph said.

Ralph leaned down and tapped on the glass with his finger. The lizard blinked.

"I'll tell you, Adam Joshua," he said, "a lizard just doesn't have much personality."

———

"Listen up, everybody," Ms. D. called out. "Company manners. The other classes are on their way."

Other classes from the school paraded by to look at the pets.

"Champion, Jump!" shouted Elliot. "Champion, Roll! Champion, Fetch!"

"What a dog!" yelled a first grader as everyone cheered and applauded.

"What tricks does your dog do?" a girl asked politely as they all crowded around to see George.

Adam Joshua had been afraid someone was going to ask that.

Elliot stood at the edge of the crowd, smirking.

"He sleeps on my stomach," Adam Joshua said, standing tall and petting George on the head so he'd feel proud.

"That's nice, Adam Joshua," another girl said, "but we meant tricks like Champion does."

Adam Joshua petted George harder.

"George is too busy for those kinds of tricks," he said. "He has too many other things on his mind."

Several kids shook their heads sadly.

"Stop dillydallying and get to work!" Sebastian said.

"The judges are coming!" Ms. D. called.

Miss Willow, a fourth-grade teacher, looked nervous.

Mrs. Jackson, the librarian, looked determined.

Dr. Mona, the veterinarian, looked like she was trying to remember how she got talked into this.

"Champion won a blue ribbon at the last dog show he was in," Elliot told them. "Just watch," he said.

Champion jumped, and fetched and died, and jumped up again to roll over. The judges cheered and applauded, and wrote things on their clipboards.

"Blue is Champion's favorite color," Elliot called after them.

———

The judges stood in front of George.

"Is there anything special you want to tell us about George?" Mrs. Jackson asked.

Adam Joshua was ready.

"He sleeps on my stomach, and he listens to all my problems, and laughs at my jokes, and takes care of Amanda Jane. He's my friend."

"Tricks?" asked Mrs. Jackson.

"Doesn't have time," said Adam Joshua.

George smiled at the judges and wagged all over.

"Well, he's a wonderful dog!" Dr. Mona said. "Healthy and loved. And isn't he sweet!"

"Really sweet." Miss Willow chuckled as she petted George too.

"Sweet," said Mrs. Jackson, writing it on her clipboard.

"Champion can be as sweet as they come!" Elliot yelled across at them.

"I need to check on Nelson, and look at some of the other pets," Adam Joshua told George after the judges had gone. "Don't worry about Champion, and don't listen to Sebastian. You were great!" he said, giving George a hug.

"I'll watch him for you, Adam Joshua," said Ralph. "It will be nice to have something to do."

———

Adam Joshua stopped first to visit Angie.

Walton Eight had lost his bow and was looking worse.

"If you're interested in hamsters," Angie

said, "I'd be happy to give you some advice."

Adam Joshua looked at Gabby's parakeet and Heidi's mouse, and he stopped to look at the nothing on the end of Lizzie's leash.

"Her name is Fang," Lizzie said proudly. "Isn't she great!"

Adam Joshua went around a corner and came eye-to-eye with a snaky-looking snake.

"This is my snake, Reba," Martha said, turning around so Adam Joshua could see the way Reba was wrapped around her shoulders.

"Would you like to hold her?"

"No thank you," Adam Joshua told Martha. "George gets jealous if I hold other people's snakes."

"I never knew that about dogs," Martha called after him, scratching her snake behind the ears.

————

Adam Joshua found Nelson standing beside Tyler's aquarium with his book.

"That's a Mexican swordtail," Nelson said, pointing to a picture in his book and then to one of Tyler's fish. They're hardy and friendly and if it was my fish," Nelson said, "I'd name him Thor."

Tyler looked at his fish and looked at Nelson.

He looked a little shy.

"Thor is a good name," he said.

———

"Listen up," Ms. D. called out. "It's award time. Everyone stand tall and proud by your pet."

Adam Joshua hurried back to stand tall and proud by George.

Elliot got busy fluffing up Champion's fur.

"There might be reporters," he said. "And Champion will look terrific when he gets his prize."

———

Mrs. Jackson, and Dr. Mona, and Miss Willow lined up in front of everyone. Ms. D. came to stand beside them.

"She's holding lots of ribbons!" everybody whispered.

"You've done a great job today!" Ms. D. said. "And we think all your pets are just won-

room. "I don't believe it," he whispered, looking awful.

Tyler was already there, taking up the center of the room. Beside him was a big aquarium full of more types of fish than Adam Joshua had known existed. There were yellow and purple and blue ones and, zipping around up in the corner, a plump red one.

Nelson didn't say anything. He took his bowl of fish over to a table in the corner, and then he stood looking at them a minute and moved the bowl to a table under the window where they could have more light. He took a big breath and looked at Adam Joshua.

"You have very nice fish, Tyler," Nelson said.

Tyler looked surprised.

"Yeah, I guess so," he said. "My parents keep buying them for me, and I guess they can be pretty interesting."

"What are their names?" Nelson asked, moving closer to the aquarium to get a better look.

"I never thought about giving them names,"

Tyler said, shrugging. "I can't even tell a lot of them apart."

Nelson looked a little sick, and went to stand by his fish at the window again.

He patted the bowl.

When Adam Joshua got back outside, there was a parrot on the table beside George. George had his paws up on the table and his nose against the parrot's cage, trying to get friendly.

"Pick up your dirty socks," said the parrot. He reached through the cage and bit George on the nose.

"Sorry," Jonesy said as George dove under the table. "This is Sebastian and he's not the nicest bird. In fact," said Jonesy, "I don't even like him much."

Adam Joshua crawled under the table and pulled out George.

"Don't talk to strangers," he said, kissing George where Sebastian had bitten him.

"Besides," Jonesy said, "for a month I tried to teach Sebastian to talk, and he wouldn't say a thing. So then my mother tried, and now that stupid bird only says what she tells him to say."

"This room is a disgrace," said Sebastian.

George lay down beside the table leg and got quiet. When Elliot got to the table across the way with his dog, Champion, George didn't even bat an eye.

"So that's your great dog," Elliot said, shaking his head. "This is going to make you feel terrible," he laughed. "Just watch."

Elliot threw a stick and Champion fetched it. Elliot said, "Roll Over!" and Champion rolled over. Elliot said, "Play Dead!" and Champion did.

"Let's see what your dog does, Adam Joshua," Elliot said, chuckling.

Adam Joshua looked at George. George curled up a little tighter and closed his eyes, and pulled his ears down over them.

"Later," said Adam Joshua. "He wants to rest right now."

"That's too bad, Adam Joshua," Elliot grinned, getting out a special brush to fluff

derful. But we thought you would like ribbons that said so too!"

"Most Imaginative Pet," Dr. Mona read off her clipboard. Lizzie walked up to get her ribbon. She happily dragged her leash behind her.

"Most Dressed-Up Cat," called Mrs. Jackson.

"Thank you," said Hanah. "And Tansy thanks you too."

"Quietest Pet," read Miss Willow.

"He should have gotten the most boring," Ralph said, getting the ribbon for his lizard, Bruno.

"Feistiest Cat," called Mrs. Jackson.

"Is that an insult?" Sidney asked, dragging up Fleabitten.

"Fanciest Fish," said Dr. Mona.

Nelson started looking worried as Tyler got his ribbon.

"Snakiest Snake," said Ms. D.

Martha went up to get her award with Reba wrapped around her neck. Ms. D. backed way up and held the ribbon at arm's length.

LIZZIE

RALPH

ADAM JOSHUA

SIDNEY

HANAH

TYLER

MARTHA

NELSON

ELLIOT

JONESY

"Most Loved Fish," said Dr. Mona.

"Terrific," said Nelson, walking forward.

"Trickiest Dog," Mrs. Jackson called out.

Adam Joshua and George started looking worried.

Elliot and Champion went up. Champion rolled over, and everyone clapped and Elliot took a bow. He looked like he was going to make a speech.

"Thank you will do it nicely," Ms. D. said.

"Thank you," said Elliot, giving Adam Joshua an Elliot look.

"George—A Best Friend And A Real Sweetie!" Ms. D. called, winking at Adam Joshua.

George smiled at everybody and everybody clapped and Adam Joshua took a bow.

"Most Talkative Bird," Ms. D. called.

"Have you changed your underwear today?" Sebastian asked her.

———

Every pet got an award, even the worms.

"Squiggliest," Nate said, proudly putting the ribbon on his worm box.

Everyone started packing up their pets to take home.

Fleabitten went charging past chasing Champion, with Sidney and Elliot close behind.

"They just keep dying," Angie said, taking Dr. Mona over to see Walton.

"Has anybody seen a snake?" Martha called.

———

"This is Alice," Adam Joshua said, taking George into the bathroom and introducing him. "She listens to me when you're not around. You two get to know each other," Adam told them, "and I'll be right back."

Adam Joshua rummaged in his desk until he found a piece of paper and a marker. He rummaged again until he found tape.

"I'm back," Adam Joshua said. Alice was in her corner waiting to listen, and George was sound asleep on the floor.

"He's usually more fun," Adam Joshua said, climbing up on the sink to reach Alice's corner, "but he's had a very busy day."

Adam Joshua taped his sign to the wall beside Alice.

"Best Spider," it said.

———

Adam Joshua carried George all the way home. George fell asleep and never woke up once.

"Julius says he was a little jealous at first," Nelson said, walking beside Adam Joshua with his fishbowl. "But then he got to know Tyler's fish and he really liked them, especially a girl fish we named Sue."

Nelson turned off toward his house.

"Julius says," Nelson called back to Adam Joshua, "that he thinks he should get out more."

Adam Joshua carried George up to his bedroom and tucked him in bed.

He took George's award out of his backpack and drew a picture of George and himself together on it and taped it up in George's Corner.

Then he took out a stick, and a ball, and an old sock, to have ready so they could start practicing tricks the minute George woke up.

The Camp-In

Usually Adam Joshua stopped to play with
George when he got home from school. They
were always so happy to see each other, they
turned it into a celebration.

But one Friday afternoon, Adam Joshua
raced past George in a hurry, barely stopping
to kiss him on the nose. George had to scurry
to keep up.

"We're going to have a camp-in," Adam
Joshua told George as he started digging in
the closet for his suitcase. George helped.

"I'm sorry you can't come," Adam Joshua

said, "but when I asked Ms. D., she said it was going to be crowded enough without dogs or lizards. Ralph asked too. I think he was hoping he would lose Bruno like Martha lost her snake, Reba."

Adam Joshua could see the handle of his suitcase sticking out from under two piles of comic books, a spaceship, half an umbrella, and George.

"It's going to be crowded because we're going to sleep in the library," Adam Joshua said. He shoved the comics, and spaceship, and umbrella out of the way and started pulling on George's leg.

"It's gotten too cold to sleep outside," he said, panting, "but we're going to have a big bonfire outside, and cook hot dogs and marshmallows, and a scary storyteller's going to come."

He got the dog and the suitcase out of the closet at the same time and collapsed on both of them.

"You hate marshmallows," he told George.

———

Adam Joshua packed his toothbrush because his mother told him to, and his comics because he wanted to, and a Space Spy because Amanda Jane came by carrying it in her mouth and dropped it in his suitcase.

Adam Joshua packed his one-eyed, one-armed, no-legged teddy bear, and then he stood looking at it for a minute, and then he took it out again. He didn't want anyone thinking he needed a baby's bear to sleep with.

What he really needed was George.

He put the bear at the bottom of his sleeping bag before he rolled it up. That way, no one would see it in his suitcase, but it would be close in case he needed it.

He had a lot of the tops of pajamas and a lot of pajama bottoms, but he didn't have any tops and bottoms that made a whole pair of pajamas anymore. Every Christmas his aunts gave him pajamas, and he usually hated them, and during the year things happened to them. George had chewed up sleeves and legs, and Adam Joshua had poured a bottle of catsup over one pajama top when he was pretending he'd been shot. Adam Joshua personally thought the stain looked very interesting, but he didn't think his mother would let him wear that top in front of all those people. He had a pair of Superman pajamas he'd gotten with his own money last year, but he'd flown them to pieces.

"I think you need to open an early Christmas present, Adam Joshua," his mother said, showing up at the bedroom with a package. "From your Aunt Dorothy."

Adam Joshua sighed. Aunt Dorothy's pajamas were usually the worst. They always had rabbits on them.

Adam Joshua opened the package. These were the most awful rabbits yet. Even Amanda Jane was too old for these rabbits.

"Those are just darling." his mother said. "Won't you look cute!"

As soon as his mother walked out of the room, Adam Joshua took the rabbit pajamas out of the suitcase and hid them under his pillow. He packed his ratty, tattered, flown-to-pieces Superman pajamas. He closed the suitcase tight in case his mother came by wanting to help him pack again.

———

Adam Joshua put pillows under his blanket and plumped them up to look like a body so that George would have a stomach to sleep on.

He sat on the suitcase and held George on his lap.

"I really want to go to the camp-in, but I really don't want to leave you alone," he said.

George looked like he was feeling the same way about Adam Joshua being gone.

"I know you'll miss me, but it's just for one night, and my mother says she'll keep a good close eye on you," Adam Joshua told George.

George looked a little worried about Adam Joshua's mother keeping such a close eye on him.

"If you need me, just tell somebody to call and I'll come in a minute," Adam Joshua said.

George looked at Adam Joshua like he had to be kidding. The only other person who could understand George was Amanda Jane, and no one else would be able to understand her.

George started giving Adam Joshua a look

to let him know he was feeling all alone and forgotten in the world.

Adam Joshua pretended not to notice.

———

"I don't know about this," Nelson said as Adam Joshua's mother drove them to the school. "My mother said she'd take care of my fish but"—Nelson glanced at Adam Joshua's mother and whispered—"you know how mothers are."

Adam Joshua sighed and didn't look at the look George was giving him.

"Adam Joshua," his mother said when he got out of the car, "I noticed you packed some stained and torn pajamas by mistake, so I took them out and put your new rabbit ones in instead." She handed him his suitcase.

"Have a wonderful night," she said, giving him a hug.

Amanda Jane waved good-bye out the car window, and George hung his head out of the window, rolled his eyes, and looked totally betrayed and rejected.

"Adam Joshua," Nelson said as they carried

their suitcases into the school, "I had no idea you liked rabbits."

———

Everyone was standing around the library looking like they weren't too sure whose idea this was, and like they weren't too sure it was such a great idea to begin with.

"I've never slept with this many people around before," Nelson whispered.

Some of the girls were already laying out their sleeping bags.

"You sleep on this side of me," Heidi told Angie. "And you sleep on that side of me," she told Lizzie.

"I talk in my sleep," Heidi told Adam Joshua. "Angie and Lizzie are my friends, so they already know all about me. But I say things in my sleep I wouldn't want a lot of other people to know."

Adam Joshua didn't think he talked in his sleep. George had never mentioned it.

"I just hope I don't snore," Sidney said.

Ms. D. walked in the door with a tall thin man. He had blue eyes and a red beard.

"This is my husband," Ms. D. said, introducing him all around.

Adam Joshua had never thought about Ms. D. having a husband. And if he had thought of it, he thought, he never would have thought of Ms. D. having a husband with a beard.

Mr. D. looked at the ceiling, and he looked at the floor, and he stood around looking shy.

"He's going to sleep on the boys' side of the room," Ms. D. said, "so if you need anything, just let him know."

Adam Joshua didn't know how he felt about camping with a stranger, but he thought if Ms. D. liked him, he was probably all right.

"I just hope nobody else snores either," said Sidney.

———

When they went outside, the night was black and crisp and cold.

"The dark is not one of my favorite things," Ms. D. said as they walked. Adam Joshua noticed she cuddled a little closer to Mr. D. and held his hand. Adam Joshua would have held her hand instead, if she'd just asked.

44

The campfire was bright and crisp and crackling.

"Isn't this great, Adam Joshua?" Gabby said, settling beside him on the ground while they roasted their frankfurters. "I love camping. Once we camped in Yellowstone and we saw bears, and once we camped in Canada and we saw moose. Of course, we probably won't see any bear or moose tonight."

Adam Joshua liked his frankfurters burnt. He held his in the fire until it caught fire, and then he let it stay on fire for a good long time.

"And once we were camping and my little brother got lost. Of course," Gabby said, "he was such a pain, I sort of thought it would be nice if he stayed lost, but my parents didn't feel that way about it."

Gabby's frankfurter caught fire too while she was talking, but Adam Joshua thought she wanted it that way.

"And I've had some really boring camping trips where it rained all the time," said Gabby. "And being with my brother in the tent in the rain is the worst thing in the world."

"Adam Joshua, that's the second blackest hot dog I've ever seen," Ms. D. said as he lined up behind her for the catsup.

"I don't know why this always seems to happen," Gabby sighed, looking at her hot dog as she lined up behind him.

"That's the blackest," said Ms. D.

———

Adam Joshua noticed that Mr. D. roasted Ms. D.'s frankfurters for her.

When Ms. D. said she was chilly, Mr. D. put his arm around her.

When he thought no one was looking, Mr. D. leaned over and gave Ms. D. a kiss on the nose.

"I think Mr. D.'s a dope," Philip muttered.

"I think he's a wise guy," said Jonesy.

"I think he's a jerk," growled Ralph.

"I really love campfires," Sidney said. "Campfires are great for singing."

"One Hundred Bottles of Root Beer on the Wall," Sidney sang.

"One Hundred Bottles of Root Beer," Ms. D. and everybody else sang along.

"One Hundred Bottles of Root Beer on the

Wall," Sidney started all over again once they ended the first song.

Everybody groaned.

"GREAT GREEN GLOBS OF GREASY GRIMY GOPHER GUTS," Sidney sang just as Adam Joshua was biting into his second hot dog.

"Hey! What's the matter?" Sidney hollered, ducking as everyone threw marshmallows at him.

Adam Joshua burned another marshmallow and offered it to Ms. D.

"Just the way I like them," Ms. D. said, licking her fingers. "By the way, take it easy with Mr. D.," she whispered. "He doesn't get much of a chance to be around kids. He's a little nervous and worried, and might need you guys to cheer him up."

Adam Joshua had been thinking Mr. D. looked a little nervous and worried.

He went over and sat down beside him. He couldn't think of anything to say.

Mr. D. looked like he didn't know what to say either.

"Nice night," Mr. D. finally said.

Adam Joshua nodded.

"Nice moon, nice stars," said Mr. D.

Adam Joshua nodded.

They both got quiet again.

Adam Joshua thought he'd cheered up Mr. D. enough.

"Nice talking to you," Mr. D. said as Adam Joshua left.

"Think I'll go cheer up Mr. D.," Nelson said on his way by.

———

"In a little while, a storyteller's coming," Ms. D. told everyone, "and we'll all cuddle down around the fire so it will be nice and spooky while she tells us ghost stories."

"I love ghost stories," said Angie, "especially if somebody loses their head. I just love ghosts without heads."

"I love ghost stories with a lot of blood and guts," said Ralph. "It's okay if the ghosts keep their heads," he said, "but the story should have a lot of blood."

"I love ghost stories about sad ladies," said Heidi.

"Dripping blood's good," said Ralph.

"I like ghost stories about ghost animals," said Martha.

"A trail of blood's terrific," said Ralph.

"My favorite ghost stories are about haunted houses," said Philip.

"Bloody footprints are always nice," said Ralph.

———

While they waited, Mr. D. got out a guitar. He sat by the fire and looked at the stars and sang a sad song. Sidney didn't know the words, but he sang along with him.

When they finished, a Gypsy was standing at the edge of the fire. She had a scarf on her head, and bracelets up and down her arms, and a long skirt that swept to the ground, and a shawl that looked like a spider's web.

"Gather 'round," Ms. D. whispered. "Our storyteller's here."

———

Everybody gathered together in a hurry. Everyone tried to get a seat as close to the fire

and as far away from the dark as possible.

"Once," the Gypsy started the story in a creaky voice, "there was a ghost."

Nelson scooted closer to Adam Joshua on one side, and they both scooted closer to Mr. D.

The Gypsy told a story about a ghost with a head, and then she told a story about a ghost without one. She told a story that had a haunted house in it, and a lot of blood.

"Yuck," Ralph whispered.

Martha raised her hand and asked for a story about a ghost animal.

Adam Joshua wished she hadn't.

The storyteller told a story about a ghost dog that came back to haunt the boy who had owned it, because the boy had been mean.

Adam Joshua didn't plan to ever let George get sick, and he didn't plan to ever let George die, and he didn't think George would ever haunt him, but then George hadn't been in the best mood when Adam Joshua left. He thought maybe they would have to have a good talk about it sometime soon.

When the Gypsy was finished, she seemed

to drift away into the night as quickly as she had come.

"That was great," Ms. D. said as they waved good-bye to the Gypsy.

Everybody nodded quietly. Some people thought it had been great, but a lot of people kept looking over their shoulders.

The fire was down to a soft glow, and it seemed to Adam Joshua the dark had gotten a lot darker.

"I think it's time for bed," Ms. D. said, yawning and stretching.

"Everybody come along," she said, leading the way.

Adam Joshua was glad Mr. D. was at the back of the line.

It was so dark a ghost could walk off with anybody.

———

"The girls sleep on the right side of the room," Ms. D. said when they got to the library, "and the guys on the left. Mr. Peters, the janitor, was nice enough to stretch a rope down the middle for us, so we'll hang some

blankets over it to give each side some privacy."

Adam Joshua had decided it was great that Mr. D. was going to sleep on their side of the library. In fact, after the ghost stories, he wished that Ms. D. had more husbands to go around.

He and Nelson put their sleeping bags as close to Mr. D.'s as they could, but since everyone else was trying to do the same, it wasn't that close.

Ms. D. and the girls went down to the classroom and bathrooms first to change into their night things.

"I don't know if anybody's interested in this . . ." Mr. D. said the minute they were gone. He pulled a bag from the bottom of his sleeping bag and dumped it open.

Out fell rubber spiders, and plastic bugs, and gruesome creepy crawlies.

All the boys jumped around and cheered and pounded Mr. D. on the back.

"I reserve the biggest spider for Ms. D., of course," said Mr. D.

"Well, of course," said Ralph.

Philip and Jonesy kept watch.

Mr. D. put the biggest spider under Ms. D.'s pillow.

"That'll drive her crazy," he said, chuckling.

Adam Joshua put a medium-sized spider under Hanah's pillow, and two plastic bugs down at the foot of Angie's sleeping bag.

"I wish I'd brought some cold spaghetti," said Philip. "One time I put cold spaghetti in my sister's bed, and it drove her nuts. She thought it was worms," he said, looking proud.

"Cold spaghetti would have been terrific," Mr. D. said, looking sad that he hadn't thought of it.

The girls came marching back through the door. Adam Joshua couldn't believe it. Angie had on a robe with clowns all over it, and she had on slippers with cow heads on the toes. Heidi had on pajamas with feet, and Lizzie was wearing a nightgown with so many ruffles you could hardly see Lizzie.

"Early Christmas presents," Angie said, sighing.

The boys marched down the hall to change.

Adam Joshua went into the bathroom and started taking off his shirt.

When he looked up, Alice was watching.

"Excuse me," he said, turning off the light and getting into his pajamas in the dark. Even in the dark he could feel the rabbits looking stupid. He put his school clothes back on over them.

"Nobody had better say a word about these pajamas," Jonesy was saying when Adam Joshua came out.

The only person who looked good in his pajamas was Elliot, but then Elliot would.

"People really look different at night, Adam Joshua," Nelson said on their way to the library. "Some people don't look like the same people at all."

The girls hooted and hollered when the boys walked in wearing their pajamas.

Mr. D. was wearing a football jersey, and a baseball cap, and Hawaiian shorts.

"Time to tuck in," Ms. D. said. And in front of everybody she walked over and kissed Mr. D. good night.

Adam Joshua had seen his father kiss his mother, and he had seen Nelson's father kiss Nelson's mother, and he had seen a lot of people on TV kiss a lot of other people. But he had never seen anyone kiss Ms. D. Since it was Mr. D. it was probably all right, but Adam Joshua wasn't sure he liked it.

He climbed into his sleeping bag and pulled it up over his head.

A lot of other people did the same.

———

The library seemed like a different place with the lights off.

"I hate the dark," Ms. D. said from the other side of the room.

"She always sleeps with the lights on," Mr. D. whispered, "but don't tell her I said so."

All the boys lay on their side of the library, chuckling into their sleeping bags, waiting for the screams to start on the girls' side.

Nothing happened.

"Ms. D. should find that big spider any time," Mr. D. whispered, "and she's going to scream like crazy. I put it where she can't miss it."

All the boys lay quiet, waiting.

Nothing happened.

Then out of the dark came a terrible, yowling, howling scream.

Adam Joshua couldn't see Mr. D., but he could feel him jump out of his sleeping bag and throw something high into the air.

Somebody turned on the lights.

Mr. D. was standing there, looking up.

A horrible, long rubber snake was hanging down from the light fixture.

All the girls were hooting and howling.

"Got a problem?" Ms. D. called.

"No problem," Mr. D. growled, smacking off the light again and leaving the snake where it hung.

"I wish she wouldn't do things like that," muttered Mr. D.

———

It got very dark. It got very quiet.

Adam Joshua pulled his feet up high in his sleeping bag, just in case Ms. D. brought extra rubber snakes.

"What the heck," Mr. D. said. He jumped up and took a running start at the curtain. He

58

gave his pillow a great dunk shot toward where Ms. D. was sleeping.

Nobody on the other side of the curtain said anything.

Somebody turned the light on.

"Excuse me," Heidi said, walking around the curtain edge with Mr. D.'s pillow. "Did you lose this?"

"Thank you," Mr. D. said politely, taking his pillow back.

"No problem at all," said Heidi.

Three pillows came sailing over the top of the curtain and landed flat on top of Mr. D.'s head.

———

Adam Joshua clobbered Heidi with his pillow, and he clobbered Martha, and Angie clobbered him.

Mr. D. kept trying to sneak up on Ms. D., but Ms. D. was too fast for him.

Adam Joshua tried sneaking up on Ms. D. himself.

"Don't worry about me," Mr. D. said as Adam Joshua stepped over him. "Save yourselves."

— Lub nie chce, panie poruczniku.

— Zastanawiałem się już nad tym, Cliff...

— Zastanowi się pan jeszcze bardziej dzięki tasiemce z podsłuchu, to jest ta druga sprawa. Wczorajsza rozmowa między pańskim stryjem a komendantem...

Wrzuciłem taśmę do magnetofonu. Była interesująca nie tylko dlatego, że pierwszy raz usłyszałem jak ci dwaj drą koty (krótkie spięcie, ale jednak):

„ — Wiesz, że przyjechał nowy nuncjusz?

— Twoi agenci zdobyli dzisiaj tę wiadomość? Telewizja już wczoraj mówiła o nim.

— I mówiła, że on chce ci dokopać?

— Skąd to wiesz?

— Moi agenci zdobyli tę wiadomość. Włoch będzie składał we wtorek listy uwierzytelniające i przy okazji poskarży się Rabonowi, że główny burdel Nolibabu nosi nazwę «Święta Trójca».

— Mój statek nosi inną nazwę.

— Jaką inną?! Przecież «Santissima Trinidad»...

— «Santissima Trinidad» to nie «Święta Trójca», tylko «Przenajświętsza Trójca»!

— Zobaczymy, czy dopisze ci takie samo poczucie humoru, kiedy ten makaroniarz wyrazi swoje oburzenie prezydentowi!

— Jons go podbechtał do tego?

— Jons umiera na raka, ma kilka dni lub tygodni przed sobą i nie rozmawia już z nikim.

— Ale ktoś podbechtał makaroniarza!

— Nie jest ważne kto, istotne jest, że we wtorek on się poskarży u tronu!

— No to należy mu ten zamysł wypukać!

— Nie, Hub, trzeba jeszcze dzisiaj zmienić nazwę statku! Nie róbmy wojny z Kościołem...

— Nie chcę wojny, lecz nazwy statku nie dam zmienić. Jons żądał tego samego i jakoś się z nim dogadałem.

— Po czym złamałeś umowę, Hub! Nie wycofałeś okrętu na pas eksterytorialny!

— Bo «Santissima Trinidad» przez prawie rok nie był burdelem, tylko remontowanym zabytkiem, a zabytku nie musiałem wycofywać! Do tego odległość od portu nie była ustalona precyzyjnie...

— Z nuncjuszem Terrafinim takie sztuczki nie przejdą! Jons umrze lada dzień i ten Włoch będzie miał wpływ na wybór nowego prymasa. A ty chcesz się z nim kłócić! I to właśnie wtedy, kiedy ja chcę mieć Kościół po mojej stronie, Flowenol!... Zmienisz nazwę statku!

— Nie zmienię nigdy!

— Hub, to nie jest prośba, to rozkaz!

— Rozkazy możesz wydawać swoim enbekom!

— Niech cię piekło weźmie!

— Niech kiedyś weźmie, ale zostaw mi jeszcze trochę czasu. Teraz chodzi o to, by makaroniarz mi nie bruździł. Powiedz Grantowi, że musi napisać artykuł wymierzony w Terrafiniego...

— Ja mam mu powiedzieć?!

— A kto? Ty mu wetknąłeś tę laleczkę ze swojej stajni i ty mu obiecałeś stołek szefa telewizji! Obiecaj mu również ministerstwo kultury, to przełamie jego strach. Artykuł ma być gotowy wieczorem i wydrukowany do siódmej rano, a ja muszę mieć jutro możność porozmawiania z Terrafinim. Macie coś na niego?

— Mamy coś na każdego, lecz ja nie chcę wojny z Watykanem, mówiłem ci już!

— Ja też ci już mówiłem, że tej wojny nie chcę. Nie będę z makaroniarzem wojował, tylko zmiękczę go jak ugotowaną nitkę spaghetti, lub złamię go jak surową nitkę spaghetti!

— Czym go złamiesz?

— Najpierw będę go zmiękczał, łagodną perswazją seksualno-teologiczną, tak jak to było z Jonsem, a jeśli ten dialog nie przyniesie skutku, to złamię go artykułem Granta.

— A gdy i to nie przyniesie skutku?

— Wówczas zagram kartami, które ty wyjmiesz z archiwum en-
beckiego. Wyjmij je do jutra, i na jutro załatw mi tę audiencję dla
dwóch osób.

— Dwóch?

— Pójdę z Nurnim. On kiedyś przejmie statek, więc musi się
uczyć jak bronić tego skarbu, dlatego wziąłem go do kardynała
Jonsa i teraz wezmę do nuncjusza.

— Jeśli tak... Dobrze, to mi jest na rękę, bandyto!.. Nie audiencja
zorganizowana przez szefa NB, tylko umówiona wizyta szefa BS-u
w związku z zagrożeniem terrorystycznym!

— Żeby Nurni był jedynym winowajcą, gdyby coś poszło źle?

— Gdyby coś poszło źle, ty będziesz jedynym prawdziwym winowajcą, on będzie kozłem ofiarnym, przyjacielu! Ja zaś nie będę
ryzykował łba dlatego, że pan Flowenol uparł się co do nazwy statku
i lubi pojedynki. Jesteś niebezpiecznym partnerem!

— Jestem szczodrym partnerem.

— Co będę miał z faktu, że finansowałeś mój plan, gdy przez
swój upór zepsujesz wszystko?

— Nie zepsuję niczego. Ja i Nurni damy sobie radę.

— Z kardynałem Terrafinim być może dasz sobie radę. Pytanie,
czy kiedyś dasz sobie radę z Nurnim! On ma pierdolca w mózgu, i
będzie miał tak długo, póki nie dostanie tej kobiety i Krimma. A ponieważ wiemy obaj, że nie dostanie ich nigdy, to obaj wiemy, że
będzie chory dożywotnio! Czy nie lepiej byłoby powiedzieć mu?

— Jeszcze nie czas. Niech czas go leczy.

— Wątpię, żeby czas go uleczył.

— A masz do niego jakieś zastrzeżenia służbowe? Jego zespół
nawala?

— Nie nawala, bo on ma pierwszorzędnych oficerów, którzy zaj-
mują się całą robotą!...".

Poza tym na taśmie nie było ciekawych informacji. Gdy się
skończyła, brzmiało mi w uszach: „mój plan", i: „obaj wiemy, że nie
dostanie ich nigdy", i: „czy nie lepiej byłoby powiedzieć mu?". Co

powiedzieć? Jaki plan? I z jakiego powodu, do cholery, miałbym
nigdy nie znaleźć Miriam i Krimma?

— Słyszałeś, Cliff? Jesteś pierwszorzędnym oficerem, który od-
wala całą robotę, a ja jestem psychiczny do kwadratu!

— Ja tego nie powiedziałem, szefie.

— Skończył się remont, macie czasu od cholery. Wyselekcjonuj
wśród naszych ludzi elitę i bierz się za Krimma!

— Taerg nie pozwolił panu ścigać Krimma, sam mi pan to mówił,
szefie.

— Dlatego teraz mówię: weź najbardziej zaufanych!

— Rozkaz, panie poruczniku!

Nowy nuncjusz watykański, kardynał Amedeo Terrafini, miał
dziwną budowę: ciało okrąglutkiego tłuściocha, a głowę i szyję kon-
dora, czyli suche, wydłużone, z wielkimi ślepiami i kłakami rzadkich
włosów. Witając stryja i mnie uprzedził, że może nam poświęcić kwadrans. Gdy wyjąłem swoją legitymację, machnął ręką:

— Nie trzeba, poruczniku. O co chodzi?

— Między innymi o bezpieczeństwo waszej eminencji, bo działa-
ją u nas bandy terrorystyczne...

— O bezpieczeństwie mojej eminencji winien pan rozmawiać z
szefem służb nuncjatury, poruczniku. O co rzeczywiście chodzi?

Był złośliwy i twardy jak wszyscy, którym biologia zrobiła kawał
dziwną anatomią, to zaś wróżyło niezłą drakę.

— Jest pewna delikatna kwestia, eminencjo, kwestia pewnego
statku. Doniesiono nam, że eminencji nie podoba się nazwa tego
statku i że eminencja chce to omówić z prezydentem, czemu prag-
niemy zapobiec, eminencjo, gdyż naszym obowiązkiem jest dbałość
o komfort psychiczny prezydenta.

— Możecie temu zapobiec zmuszając właściciela statku do zmiany jego nazwy lub do zmiany jego funkcji. To drugie byłoby nawet
lepsze.

— Właścicielem okrętu jest ten pan.

Wskazałem Huberta, który się ukłonił:

— Jestem Hubert Flowenol, eminencjo.

— To pańska sprawa. Czego pan sobie życzy, panie Flowenol?

— Życzę sobie wpłynąć na waszą eminencję.

— Wpłynąć? Jak?

— Siłą argumentów.

— Słownych argumentów?

— A można innych?

— Nie można, nie jestem łapownikiem.

— Więc retorycznych.

— Siłą argumentów retorycznych jest niepodważalna logika. Stać pana na nią?

— Zawsze.

— Tak pan mówi?... Ma pan niepełny kwadrans, żeby tego dowieść, panie Flowenol.

— Eminencjo, na moim statku prowadzona jest wielostronna działalność o charakterze rekreacyjno-rozrywkowym. Gry komputerowe, gry hazardowe...

— Kościół nie pochwala żadnych gier hazardowych, panie Flowenol!

— Eminencjo, nic nie słyszałem, by Kościół ekskomunikował księcia Rainiera, chociaż z Monte Carlo do Watykanu jest dużo bliżej niż z Watykanu do Nolibabu! Pozwoli eminencja, że skończę. Kasyno, restauracja, sauna, taniec, muzyka, filmy...

— A te kobiety?

— To hostessy, które umilają czas gościom mojego statku.

— Miał pan argumentować, nie kłamać, panie Flowenol! To płatne dziwki, i każdy wie, że na pańskim statku jest dom schadzek, a taki dom to hańba, obraza człowieczeństwa!

— Człowieczeństwa? Jeśli chce eminencja zapoznać się z hańbą autentyczną, to radzę zwiedzić Tajlandię i popatrzeć na miliony małych dzieci zmuszanych do zawodowej prostytucji ciężkim biciem i przypalaniem ognikami papierosów! Zobaczy eminencja, co to jest człowieczeństwo!

— Mówisz o barbarzyńcach i poganach, o Azjatach! Mów dalej, masz jeszcze dziewięć minut.

— Mówię o nas! Każdy z tych kilkuletnich chłopców i każda z tych kilkuletnich panienek obsługuje dziesięciu klientów podczas jednej doby. I nie jest to klientela azjatycka. To są Niemcy, Szwedzi, Francuzi, Anglicy, jankesi i inne chluby cywilizacji zachodniej. Masowo przyjeżdżają do Pattayi i do Bangkoku, by rżnąć ośmioletnich! Na moim statku wykluczone jest pedofilstwo, lecz w spelunkach Nolibabu takie rzeczy się uprawia, a o krucjacie kościelnej przeciw nim jak dotąd nie słyszałem!

— Kościół nie jest policją obyczajową!

— Kościół w tym państwie współrządzi!

— Siedem minut, trzydzieści sekund!

— A ponieważ współrządzi i nic przeciwko temu nie robi, to jest współwinny! Zresztą nie tylko w tej sprawie, którą ostatecznie możemy uznać za margines deprecjacji człowieczeństwa. Również wtedy, gdy deprawowana jest cała młodzież naszego kraju. A jest deprawowana, eminencjo, bo chociaż w każdej naszej szkole mamy lekcje religii, to w mediach mamy pogadanki o tak zwanej kontrkulturze, wolnej miłości et cetera!

— Kościół walczy z tym, panie Flowenol. Sześć i pół minuty!

— W pisemkach kościelnych, których nikt nie czyta, i kazaniami, które wierni puszczają mimo uszu! Chodzi o coś zupełnie innego — o twardą rękę władzy! Ta władza jest ślepa i głucha, lecz niezupełnie — jest selektywnie ślepa i głucha. Uprawia cenzurę polityczną, a obyczajowej nie uprawia, co ma stanowić dowód naszej przynależności do świata kultury Zachodu. Niedawno w serii młodzieżowej jednego z wydawnictw ukazał się poradnik seksu oralnego. Czy Kościół kiwnął przeciwko temu palcem? Czy ukarano lub choćby tylko napiętnowano deprawatora? Nie, eminencjo! Więc deprawator będzie dalej robił to, co umie robić, będzie deprawował, i bardzo dobrze, w końcu tak być powinno, każdy powinien robić tylko to, na czym się zna, bo w przeciwnym razie zapanuje triumf niekompetencji. Szkoda, że Kościół nie jest tego samego zdania i nie wypełnia swoich obowiązków!

yawning. "Move your sleeping bag over here. Bring your teddy bear."

Adam Joshua looked around. Everybody had a stuffed animal.

Nate had three stuffed dogs. They were all named Windberg. Philip had an alligator. Nelson had a stuffed fish. Sidney had a skunk.

"Gee," said Mr. D., looking around. "I wish I'd known. I wanted to bring my stuffed moose, Morose, but Ms. D. wouldn't let me."

———

Somebody turned off the lights.

It got dark. It got quiet.

Sidney snored.

Ralph muttered about blood as he slept.

Adam Joshua dreamed that he was caught in the Gypsy's spiderweb shawl, and that he was going to be stuck there all his life, listening to ghost stories.

Mr. D. let out a howling, yowling, blood-curdling scream.

By the time somebody turned on the lights, Mr. D. was standing on top of a library table, and three boys who had been sleeping near him were up on tables too.

Everybody from the girls' side came hurrying around the curtain, and they all stopped in their tracks.

"My goodness!" Ms. D. said, staring at Mr. D.'s sleeping bag.

"Reba!" Martha yelled.

There was a stampede as everyone else hurried over to climb up on library tables with Mr. D.

Martha pulled Reba the rest of the way out of Mr. D.'s sleeping bag and wrapped the snake around her neck.

"Did that bad man scare you, sweetie?" she asked, kissing Reba on the nose.

"She's been lost since Pet Day," Ms. D. told Mr. D. while helping him down from the table. "She must have been staying in the library, and decided to hide in your sleeping bag during the pillow fight."

"I'd like to go home now," Mr. D. said. "I really need Morose."

Ms. D. checked Mr. D.'s sleeping bag for more snakes, and she tucked him in.

She made Martha take Reba down to the classroom, and she made everybody get into

their sleeping bags and stay there.

"No more talking," she said firmly. "No more screaming."

"No more snakes," Mr. D. said, shuddering.

Adam Joshua and Nelson moved their sleeping bags as far away from Mr. D. as they could.

———

The lights weren't off ten minutes before there was a truly terrible howling yowling yelping.

Everybody jumped up screaming, and everybody ran into everybody else in the dark, until somebody turned the lights on.

Everybody glared at Mr. D.

"It wasn't me," he said. "Honest!"

"It sounded like it came from outside the window," Ms. D. said, leading the way.

Mr. D. and a few others crept along behind.

The howling started again, but it stopped the minute Ms. D. raised the shade.

"Smart ghost," Mr. D. whispered. "Nobody's going to haunt Ms. D."

"Adam Joshua," Ms. D. said, laughing, "this ghost looks awfully familiar."

The ghost looked just like George. And George looked just like a dog who had found his way to school all by himself and was feeling pretty proud of it.

"I wish Julius could have come too," Nelson sighed.

Adam Joshua went to the office to call his father, and then he went outside with Mr. D. to wait with George.

George looked pleased to see him.

"I can't believe it!" Adam Joshua hollered at George. "I told you no dogs were allowed, and I told you I'd be back, and I told you not to worry!"

George stopped looking pleased, and started looking mad about the hollering.

"I don't even want to talk about it!" Adam Joshua yelled. "We'll discuss it when I get home."

"Really?" Mr. D. said, interested. "No kidding?"

"Besides," Adam Joshua said, winding down, "it's a lot quieter at home. You'd never get any sleep around here."

"Isn't that the truth," yawned Mr. D.

Adam Joshua's father showed up with his coat on over his pajamas, and he looked half asleep and half mad as he scooted George into the car.

Adam Joshua glared good-bye at George, and George glared good-bye at Adam Joshua.

"I'm sorry," Adam Joshua told Mr. D. as they walked back into the school. "He's not like most dogs. He's my friend, and he worries about me."

"Don't worry," Mr. D. said. "If my moose, Morose, wasn't stuffed, he'd be a worrier too."

When they got back to the library, everybody was sitting propped up against the bookcases, trying to stay awake. They all looked exhausted.

"We're going to sleep with the lights on," Mr. D. announced.

"Thank goodness," said Ms. D.

Adam Joshua tried sleeping with his eyes open for as long as he could. He could see Mr. D. doing the same.

———

For the rest of the night, the Gypsy chased Adam Joshua through his dreams, carrying a ghost head under her arm. A mad ghost George followed behind singing "Green Greasy Gopher Guts."

In the morning Adam Joshua had never been so glad to wake up in his life.

When he opened his eyes, Ms. D. was standing there looking down at Mr. D. and smiling.

Mr. D. was sound asleep in his sleeping bag. Ralph was sound asleep in Mr. D.'s sleeping bag with his fingers wrapped through Mr. D.'s beard. Sidney, Jonesy, and Nate were doing their best to be in Mr. D.'s bag too.

Adam Joshua thought Mr. D. had gotten the hang of having kids pretty fast.

"He did just fine," Adam Joshua whispered to Ms. D.

"Yeah, he did, didn't he?" Ms. D. whispered back with a smile.

———

"Pancakes for breakfast," Mr. D. said, setting up a griddle and paper plates on a table in a corner of the cafeteria.

"Animal pancakes my specialty," Mr. D. said, pulling a chef's hat and flowered apron out of a sack.

Mr. D. made rabbit pancakes and pig pancakes, and pancakes shaped like every animal Adam Joshua could think of.

"This elephant has two trunks," Hanah said, standing in line for the syrup.

"It's a new style," said Mr. D., flipping a fish pancake onto Nelson's plate. "It just came out this year."

"What will you have, Adam Joshua?" Mr. D. asked, putting more butter on the griddle. "And would you like it burnt like your marshmallows?"

"A dog," said Adam Joshua, "not burnt."

"Any dog we know?" Mr. D. asked, scooping up the batter.

"But not a ghost," said Adam Joshua. "And with a head."

Mr. D. made a pancake that looked a lot like George. It had three ears, but Adam Joshua didn't think George would mind.

"That's great, Adam Joshua," said Ralph, going back for seconds. "I asked for a dog too," he said. "I really didn't want a pancake that looked like my lizard."

"Mr. D. made a very nice pancake that

looked like my snake, Reba," Martha said. "He said to tell her that he doesn't hold a grudge."

When everyone was so full of pancakes no one could move, somebody started applauding Mr. D. and everyone joined in.

Mr. D. took his chef's hat off, made a great, sweeping bow, and got his beard in the bowl of pancake batter.

"That guy's terrific," Philip said.

"That guy's swell," said Jonesy.

"I always said he was great," said Ralph.

Everybody cleaned up, and picked up, and packed up.

"If you have a minute," Adam Joshua heard Mr. D. whispering to Philip, "I'd like to talk to you about the spaghetti you put in your sister's bed."

"I did not say that in my sleep!" Heidi yelped. "I'd never tell anybody that!" she said. "Not even asleep!"

"How else would I know?" Angie said. "But for twenty-five cents, I won't tell anybody."

"Make that fifty cents," said Lizzie.

"I don't know, Adam Joshua," Nelson said, yawning. "I feel like I've been away from home for three nights." He yawned some more. "And I feel like I didn't sleep the other two nights either."

Adam Joshua went to find Mr. D. to say good-bye. He found him asleep in the corner, with the chef's hat pulled down over his eyes.

"We'd better let him sleep," Ms. D. whispered to Adam Joshua. "He's had a rough night."

"Has anybody seen Reba?" Martha called out.

———

Everybody piled into cars and waved good-bye to everybody else.

"I'm going to sleep as soon as I get home," Nelson said. "I hope my fish stay quiet."

"I want to go to sleep, but I can't go to sleep because I'm going to a football game with my dad," said Philip. "I'll sleep in church with my dad tomorrow instead."

"That stupid snake is missing again," said Angie. "And she'd better not come crawling out of my sleeping bag when I get home."

Everybody who'd been packing their sleeping bags into cars stopped and stood looking at them for a minute.

Sidney was already in the backseat of his car with his sleeping bag. He climbed out and put the bag up front with his mother instead.

———

Nelson got into the front seat beside Adam Joshua's mother. Adam Joshua got into the backseat beside Amanda Jane and George.

"I don't know, Adam Joshua," Nelson said, yawning. "I think today's going to seem like a long day."

Amanda Jane shrieked hello. George glared and turned his back.

Adam Joshua nodded.

He had a feeling it was going to seem like a long day too.

The Fall Fling

George was still so mad about missing the camp-in, Adam Joshua hated to tell him about the Fall Fling.

"But it's really a lot of work, rather than just fun," he told George. "It's how we help make money to buy things for the school," he said. "This year we're buying a new computer. It's important."

George didn't look all that impressed.

"Besides," Adam Joshua said, sighing, "you wouldn't believe how hard we'll have to work to get ready by Saturday. And every time something like this comes up, we think we're going to get out of some of our regular work. But Ms. D. says we just have to work double time to get everything done. Ms. D. makes us work harder than any teacher I've ever had."

George didn't look the least bit sympathetic.

"Really!" Adam Joshua said.

George looked him right in the eye.

"Okay, the Fall Fling's a whole lot of fun too," Adam Joshua said.

He never could lie to George.

———

"You have a decision to make," Ms. D. told them Monday morning at school. "Every year this class handles the Bean Bag Pitch at the Fall Fling."

A lot of people groaned. The Bean Bag Pitch wasn't anybody's idea of fun. Nobody knew why they kept it around.

"That's what I thought you'd say." Ms. D. laughed. "So I had another idea for you to think about."

Everybody got very quiet and sat up a little straighter. Ms. D.'s ideas were always worth listening to.

"A lot of schools have started having Old West jails at their festivals," Ms. D. told them. "And I wondered if you might like to be the sheriffs of the Fall Fling. People would pay us to arrest their friends and put them into our jailhouse for a few minutes. It's a lot of fun, and it makes a lot of money."

Everybody started cheering and talking at once.

"That's what I thought you'd say too," Ms. D. said, satisfied.

The principal, Mrs. Rodriguez, stuck her head in the door during math.

"I just wanted to remind you about the Talent Show," she said. "It always starts off the Fall Fling, and we'll be having auditions for it this week. Anybody who'd like to try out, please get your act together and we'll see you Thursday after school."

She waved good-bye and her head disappeared.

Adam Joshua sighed. He'd been hoping that somehow he'd get talented before this week came, but so far he hadn't.

"I'm going to have an exotic snake act," said Martha. "I'm teaching Reba to curl down in a basket and come up swaying when I play for her."

"Flute?" asked Ms. D.

"Kazoo," said Martha.

"A lot of people will pay a lot of money to watch Champion do his tricks," Elliot said. "He's going to be the star of the show."

Adam Joshua sighed a little harder, and felt a little worse.

"The only trick I want to see right now is all of you getting back to work," said Ms. D.

"I was afraid she'd remember," grumbled Sidney.

———

"I'm going to do my magic act, Adam Joshua," Nelson said on their walk home. "If you want, you can be my assistant. You can help me do card tricks, and hat tricks, and I've been practicing sawing things in half, so I'll saw you in half."

Adam Joshua had been worrying for weeks about something to do for the Talent Show.

78

Still, he didn't think getting sawed in half by Nelson was the answer.

"But I'll let you know," he said, waving good-bye.

———

"So, I can't think of anything to do," Adam Joshua told George when they got up to Adam Joshua's room.

Out his window he could see Nelson over in his bedroom practicing magic for his fish.

"I'd like to be in the Talent Show, but I'm not very talented at anything. I don't sing very well, and I don't play the piano or anything, and every time I try to do magic with Nelson, his tricks work and mine fall apart."

George looked really depressed about it.

"Champion is going to do all his tricks, and Elliot says he'll be the star of the show."

George looked guilty.

"Never mind," Adam Joshua said, and he told George a joke to cheer him up.

It was about an elephant and an astronaut.

George wasn't the kind to laugh out loud, but Adam Joshua could tell he thought it was hilarious.

George tilted his head to listen, and he wagged his tail, and he smiled a lot and chuckled a little. When Adam Joshua finished, George barked for more.

"That's it!" Adam Joshua told George. "Wait here a minute."

Adam Joshua went into his closet. If he stayed in there long enough, he could find just about anything he wanted. Of course, he was exhausted by the time he did, but it was usually worth the hunt.

"This is great!" Adam Joshua said, coming out with a flowered hat and a pair of glasses with a funny nose and a mustache attached.

He put the glasses on George, and then he cut spaces in the hat for George's ears and put that on him too.

George didn't look all that thrilled about it. Still, he'd gotten used to all sorts of things happening around Adam Joshua, so he left the hat and glasses on.

Adam Joshua told George a joke about a boy and an alligator.

George loved it.

Adam Joshua told George a joke about a piano tuner and a firefly.

That joke was so funny, it nearly cracked George up.

Adam Joshua practiced telling George more jokes, and George practiced listening for a long time.

It was perfect.

"We're going to be a hit!" Adam Joshua said, hugging George—hat, nose, and all.

———

"I practiced sawing a stuffed elephant in half last night, Adam Joshua," Nelson told him the next morning on the way to school. "I did the sawing-in-half part just great, but I'm still working on the part where I put the stuffing back in. I'll probably do a lot better with a person," he said.

"No thank you, Nelson," Adam Joshua said with a shudder. "I've already decided on an act I'm going to do."

"It's probably just as well," Nelson said sadly. "I already feel bad about the elephant, but I'd feel really bad if I couldn't put your stuffing back."

They skipped recess to work on the jail. The librarian, Mrs. Jackson, and Mr. D. helped out over lunch.

"Except he's terrible help!" everybody whispered.

Mr. D. tried to add a porch, a deck, and a skylight to the jail.

"It doesn't even have a roof," Ms. D. reminded him.

"Great!" Mr. D. said, getting ready to climb up on top of the jail. "First I'll build a roof, and then I'll add a skylight."

Mr. D. tried to add an attic, and a basement, and a TV room to the jail.

"And it still needs a skylight," he told Ms. D.

Ms. D. finally had to take Mr. D.'s hammer away.

"Thank goodness," said Mrs. Jackson, unbuilding the bookshelves Mr. D. had built.

When they weren't building a jail, or doing all the school stuff Ms. D. kept giving them to do, everybody worked hard to get ready for the Talent Show.

Adam Joshua ran home each day after school to practice with George.

He kept a list of the jokes George thought were the funniest. George really loved jokes about elephants. Adam Joshua thought most dogs probably did.

"The sawing-in-half still isn't working out, Adam Joshua," said Nelson. "I just lost a stuffed alligator too."

"This is a great act," Jonesy said at recess. "Watch this!"

He sat down and Sidney came and sat in his lap.

"I'm Jonesy," said Jonesy. "I'm a ventriloquist, and this is my dummy, Sidney. Say 'Hello,' Sidney."

"Hello," said Sidney.

"This dummy is really dumb," said Jonesy. He knocked on Sidney's head. "This dummy is really a blockhead."

"Hello, again," said Sidney.

"This dummy is so dumb," said Jonesy. He

83

pounded on Sidney's head. "Go ahead, Sidney, tell them how dumb you are!"

"I'm not dumb enough to stay around for this," Sidney said, standing up and walking away.

———

"Talent Show auditions this afternoon," Mrs. Rodriguez said, popping her head in the door Thursday morning.

"I guess I'm going to have to skip the sawing," Nelson sighed.

Adam Joshua ran home right after school to get George. George remembered the way to school so well that Adam Joshua had to race to keep up.

Nelson was already onstage when they got there.

Nelson did card tricks, and some tricks with a handkerchief, and then he pulled a small fishbowl out of his hat.

"I think it's much more exciting than a rabbit," he told the judges.

———

Martha went next. She carried her basket onstage and sat down in front of it with her kazoo.

TALENT
SHOW
AUDITIONS
THURSDAY
PM

She hummed into the kazoo and the lid of the basket stayed down.

She hummed a little louder, and the lid still stayed down.

She opened the edge of the lid to peek in, and Reba slithered up out of the basket and right across the stage, then went off toward the judges.

The judges scattered in a hurry, and it took Martha ten minutes to catch Reba, and another five for the judges to settle down.

"We'll try it again," Martha said, sitting down in front of the basket with the kazoo.

"I'm sorry, Martha," Miss Willow said, still trying to catch her breath, "but we've just discovered a rule that says there can't be any snakes in the Talent Show."

"Well, for Pete's sake," Martha grumbled, packing up her kazoo and basket. "I wish somebody had told me sooner. This sort of thing makes Reba very nervous."

———

Angie went onstage dressed in a skirt that swept to the ground and a shawl that looked like a spider's web. She had a scarf on her head, and so many bracelets up and down her arm, she clanked when she walked.

"I'm going to tell you a ghost story," Angie said in a spooky, shivery voice.

She did fine at the start of the story, and okay in the middle, but somewhere toward the end she got totally lost.

"Mmm," Angie said, standing there, fingering her shawl. "Somebody loses their head, and somebody else dies, and there's a whole lot of blood, but I can't remember whose."

The judges waited patiently.

"Never mind," Angie said, walking off the stage. "It'll probably be on television sometime anyway."

———

Adam Joshua walked onto the stage with George.

George wore his glasses with the nose and mustache, and his flowered hat. A couple of the judges chuckled.

George looked a little embarrassed to be seen in public like that, but he trusted Adam Joshua.

Adam Joshua told George his best jokes,

just like he did when they were home alone without people watching.

George listened and laughed just like he always did.

The judges laughed a lot, and applauded for Adam Joshua and George when they finished up.

"You were great!" Adam Joshua said, hugging George when they got backstage.

"That's the dumbest thing I ever saw," Elliot smirked, shoving his way toward the stage with Champion.

"Adam Joshua," said Nelson, "that was really good. But if your act doesn't get chosen for the Talent Show, and you don't want to let me saw you in half, could I use George to saw in half instead?"

———

By Friday the whole school was busy and bustling.

Mrs. Rodriguez's head kept popping in the door to tell them things, and it seemed like she was always in three places at once.

"Once we've flung fall, I'm taking a long

winter's nap," Adam Joshua heard her tell Ms. D.

The jail was looking terrific.

"This is the best jail we've ever built!" Sidney said.

"It's the only jail we've ever built," said Angie.

"It's still the best," Jonesy said, "except we should have put in a tunnel. The jails on television always have ways to tunnel out."

"No tunnels," said Ms. D.

"A dungeon with a skylight would have been terrific," Mr. D. grumbled.

"Also stale water with moldy bread," added Jonesy.

———

"The list for the Talent Show is up," Angie called out on their way back to their room.

"Rats!" she told them as everybody crowded around. "I didn't make it."

A lot of people said "Rats!" A lot of people didn't make it.

"Of course, I did," Elliot said smugly, looking around to make sure everyone noticed.

"So did I!" Nelson said, sounding terrific about it. "Even without the sawing."

"And Adam Joshua," added Nelson, pointing. "Look!"

"Adam Joshua and George," it said. "A Comedy Team."

Everyone pounded Adam Joshua on the back and shook his hand and said "Congratulations!" and meant it.

Almost everybody.

"I can't believe the judges were that dumb," said Elliot.

———

"I knew we were good," Adam Joshua told George in bed that night. "But I didn't know we were that good.

"They only put really great in the Talent Show," he told George. "We were really great!"

George fell asleep while Adam Joshua was congratulating him.

"We were really, absolutely, truly terrifically great!" said Adam Joshua.

He hoped success wouldn't go to George's head.

On Friday Ms. D. handed out sheriff's stars for everybody.

Everybody cheered and carried on.

"You'll work in teams, and you'll each get a turn to be sheriff," Ms. D. told them. "And you'll all get plenty of chances to help out as deputies."

"And we can form a posse," said Jonesy. "To go after the really bad guys who won't come."

"You may have to form a few posses at that," Ms. D. laughed.

Adam Joshua felt like a sheriff the minute he put on the star. He was really glad Ms. D. had gotten one for him.

He had one almost like it at home, but he would have hated to go into his closet and try to find it.

"Tomorrow's a big day," Ms. D. said. "Everybody be here on time for the Talent Show, and good luck to our special people who are going to be in it!"

Everybody cheered and applauded, and

Adam Joshua tried to look pleased and not panicked about the Talent Show.

"Some of us are going to need a lot of luck," Elliot said, smirking clear across the room at Adam Joshua.

———

The Saturday morning of the Fall Fling was bright and blue, and crisp and perfect. Adam Joshua thought maybe he could start enjoying it as soon as the Talent Show was over.

At school, Adam Joshua's parents took their places in the audience. It was a huge audience.

"Don't be nervous, worried, or scared," Adam Joshua told George as they went backstage. George didn't look the least bit nervous, worried, or scared.

Elliot went by fluffing up Champion.

"Terrified's okay," Adam Joshua told George.

———

A fifth-grade girl opened the Talent Show by singing a song about fall. It had a bunch of leaves in it. Another girl played jazz on the piano, and a fourth grader tap-danced with a twirling baton.

They were all great, which was a whole lot better than Adam Joshua thought he and George were going to be.

"I've forgotten every joke I know," he told George.

Elliot went on and Champion did everything Champion knew how to do, and Elliot took the longest bow of the show.

"I've forgotten every joke you know too," Adam Joshua told George.

Nelson went next, and he was so nervous he nearly dropped his fishbowl. He pulled out a bouquet of roses when he said it was going to be a flag, but other than that he did fine.

"It's really scary out there," Nelson said as he came off the stage.

Adam Joshua was really sorry he'd ever thought of this.

"But we have to do it," he told George, putting George's hat and glasses on for him. "Everybody's counting on us."

People started laughing the minute they saw George. George sat down and looked at Adam

Joshua. Adam Joshua tried not to look at the audience. He just looked at George and started in.

One thing about George, no matter how many times he heard a joke, he still appreciated it.

The more jokes Adam Joshua told, the more George listened and barked, and the more people in the audience laughed.

Adam Joshua threw in a lot of elephant jokes for George. He thought it was too bad there weren't more dogs in the audience to enjoy them.

Before they knew it, they were finished and taking a bow.

"You were great, Adam Joshua," Nelson said as they came off the stage. People were still laughing and applauding.

"Even longer than for Champion," Adam Joshua whispered to George.

"They're just being polite," growled Elliot.

After the show Adam Joshua's parents hugged him, and Nelson's parents hugged him. And Ms. D. hugged him, which he wasn't expecting, and which came as quite a surprise.

Adam Joshua hugged George.

"We were terrific!" he whispered in George's ear. George yawned a little because listening to that many jokes can wear a dog out, but he brightened up the minute somebody walked by with a hot dog.

"You were the star of the show," Adam Joshua said, putting George back in the car so his parents could take him home.

George stiffened up and looked at Adam Joshua like he had to be kidding.

"I know. I'm sorry," Adam Joshua said, "but I have to stay here and work at the jail and dogs aren't allowed in the gym so you can't stay. I'm not part of the cleanup crew though, so I'll be home early.

"Not many sheriffs had dogs," Adam Joshua called after George as he waved good-bye.

George didn't look back. Adam Joshua knew what he was thinking.

Not many stars got sent home just when they were beginning to have a good time.

———

Adam Joshua couldn't believe how great the jail looked in the center of the gym.

"Except what I can't believe is that Ms. D. put that rocking chair in it," moaned Jonesy. "No moldy bread, no chains, no tunnel, but a rocking chair!"

"Ms. D. said a lot of the teachers were worried about getting thrown in jail," Angie told Adam Joshua. "And they said if they did get thrown in jail, it had better be worth the trip."

"Ms. D. said we don't want a prison riot on our hands," said Angie.

———

Philip and Jonesy were taking turns as the sheriff first, and the entire class hung around waiting to be deputies.

"Shoo!" Ms. D. told most of them, laughing. "Go have a fall fling, and have fun with the games until it's your turn.

"Good grief!" she said, hurrying over to where Philip and Jonesy were tackling their first prisoner.

"But I thought the handcuffs were a great idea," Jonesy complained as Ms. D. helped the third-grade teacher, Mr. Jarvis, to his feet and dusted him off.

———

There was a lot of fall flinging going on around the gym.

"Look, Adam Joshua," Nelson said. "There's a real magician here! Maybe he knows about the sawing stuff." Nelson hurried off toward the magician.

Adam Joshua headed over to where the races were starting.

The turtle race was first. A big turtle named Tank won because he crawled right over two smaller turtles on his way to the finish line.

A little frog named Skipit won the frog race because he was the only one who stayed on the track. Then everyone hurried around the gym for a few minutes gathering up frogs.

"There's one in here," Mr. Jarvis called, stopping the rocking chair just in time. "I always thought jails were supposed to have rats."

All the hamsters stayed in the next race, and except for Walton Eight, they all scurried for the food at the finish line. Walton sprawled halfway down the track, and lay there panting while other hamsters ran across him.

"I think he probably needs more vitamins," Angie told Adam Joshua.

Nelson came back from the magician, sadly shaking his head.

"He said sawing-in-half is still a mystery to him," Nelson said. "He said he's lost a lot of stuffed animals that way too."

They stopped for a minute to catch a fugitive frog hopping by.

"That magician says he has a whole closet full of leftover stuffing," Nelson sighed.

———

Nelson tried all the games twice, and then he settled down in front of the Ring Toss because every time he won, he won a goldfish.

Adam Joshua tried a few games, but mostly he cheered for Nelson and saved his money.

"Adam Joshua," said Nelson, stacking his bags of fish carefully in a corner, "I've already done about twenty things, and you've only done a few. I know you brought more money than that."

"I've done what I wanted to do, Nelson,"

said Adam Joshua. "And I'm saving my money for something I want to do more."

"I can't think of anything anybody would want to do more than win fish," Nelson said, heading for the Ring Toss again.

Adam Joshua had been keeping his eye on the fortune-teller, Gypsy Jade. Finally, he went over and gave her a quarter to tell his future for him.

"Either your future's very cloudy or this hand is very dirty," she told him when she started to read his palm. Adam Joshua went to wash his hands and came back.

"Much clearer," said Gypsy Jade. "You're going to travel a lot, and have a long life, and be tall, dark, and handsome, and rich and famous."

Adam Joshua was glad to hear it.

"Will I have my dog, George, for all of it?" he asked, worried.

The fortune-teller looked closely at his palm.

"Missed a line," she said. "It says you'll always have your dog, and he'll be rich and famous too."

"We're a comedy team," Adam Joshua told her, "so that's probably why."

Adam Joshua walked away satisfied. He wanted to save most of his money, but that was one of the best quarters he'd ever spent.

"Adam Joshua," said Nelson, going by with more bags, "my boss fish, Julius, is going to be very excited when I get home."

———

It was time for Angie and Adam Joshua to be sheriffs together.

They both pinned on their stars.

"Howdy, Ma'am," drawled Adam Joshua.

"Howdy, Pardner," drawled Angie.

"Angie, you go first," Ms. D. said, flipping a coin.

"Freeze, Sleaze!" Angie said, pointing her gun finger at Adam Joshua.

Mr. Jarvis went by and put a quarter into the jail box.

"The principal, Mrs. Rodriguez," he said, chuckling.

"Good grief!" said Angie, looking scared.

She walked up to Mrs. Rodriguez very slowly, and tapped her on the arm.

"Excuse me, Ma'am," Angie said politely. "You're under arrest."

"Goody!" Mrs. Rodriguez said, beating Angie back to the jail.

She sank into the rocking chair with a sigh, and pulled a paperback mystery out of her purse.

"This is the first time I've had a chance to sit down for days," she said happily. "How long am I in for?"

"Ten minutes," Angie said, locking the door.

Mrs. Rodriguez dug in her purse.

"Make it twenty," she said, handing Angie a quarter through the bars.

———

"It's your turn next, Adam Joshua," Angie told him. "I didn't know being a sheriff could make a person so nervous."

Adam Joshua leaned against the jail door, and tried to look Western and tough.

Somebody went by after a frog.

Nelson went by with more goldfish.

Sidney went by on his way to wash his hands.

"That fortune-teller, Gypsy Jade, said my

future was looking very murky," he said.

Mr. D. came by and dropped a quarter in the jail box.

"Ms. D., please," he told Adam Joshua.

Of all the people Adam Joshua thought he'd get to arrest, he'd never thought once about Ms. D. He wasn't sure he could do it.

"Sure you can," Mr. D. told him. "You're the law. What you say goes."

"Only if Ms. D. says so," said Adam Joshua.

Ms. D. was helping out at the refreshment stand.

"You're under arrest, if you don't mind," Adam Joshua told her.

"Oh, I am, am I?" Ms. D. growled, winking at him. "And I don't suppose you're going to tell me who paid to lock me up?"

"Confidential," Adam Joshua told her.

"That's who I thought it was," said Ms. D.

Once Ms. D. was locked up tight, Mr. D. came by.

"Howdy, Jailbird," he said. He leaned against the bars, crossed his arms, and whistled a mournful little tune. Then he sauntered off, trying to look innocent.

"Excuse me," Ms. D. said, handing Angie a quarter. "Please put this in the box and go arrest Mr. D. You may need a lot of help," Ms. D. called after her. "Take a posse!"

Angie grabbed Mr. D. by one arm, and Adam Joshua grabbed him by the other arm, and Heidi grabbed him around the leg.

"You're under arrest," Angie said. "Start hopping."

Mr. D. hopped his way over to the jail, and six other people helped lock him up.

"Howdy, Jailbird, yourself," Ms. D. said, giving Mr. D. a little kiss on the cheek.

Mr. D. cuddled down happily in the jail with Ms. D.

"I should have thought of this sooner," he said.

Sidney and Heidi came to take over for their turn as sheriffs.

"Try to get to arrest Mr. D.," Angie said, handing over the keys. "That's the most fun thing here."

———

Adam Joshua found Nelson and got back to the fling.

The gym was getting packed.

Everybody played games, and ate hot dogs, and went to see the fortune-teller.

A lot of people went by on the way to wash their hands.

Nelson bought raffle tickets, and put some in the box in front of a skateboard, and some more in the box for a tape player.

Jonesy had donated his parrot, Sebastian, to the raffle. Ralph had donated his lizard, Bruno.

No one was trying to win either one of them.

"I can't believe it," said Jonesy.

"Me too, either," said Ralph.

"Homework first," said Sebastian. "No TV. No telephone. No comics."

"No wonder," sighed Jonesy.

———

Mr. D. was the only adult Ms. D. would let everybody arrest the way they wanted to, so everybody arrested Mr. D. all the time.

"He's our biggest money-maker," Heidi told Ms. D.

"I'm glad to hear it," Ms. D. said.

"I'm making extra money renting out my

handcuffs," Jonesy told her, "but we're only using them on Mr. D."

"Adam Joshua," Ralph said, following him around the gym, "I'd be happy to buy a raffle ticket for you, so you could win Bruno. No one else has bought a ticket for him, so you'll probably win."

"Sorry," Adam Joshua told Ralph, "but I don't think George would get along well with a lizard."

"Smart dog," sighed Ralph.

"Excuse me," said Heidi, tapping Adam Joshua on the arm.

When he turned around, somebody threw a rope over him and three people jumped him.

"You're under arrest," Heidi told him as they dragged him toward the jail.

Adam Joshua had pretty well figured that out.

"It's just for ten minutes, Adam Joshua," Angie said, stopping by to look at him behind bars. "That's all I could afford. You worked so hard to put everybody else in jail, I thought you might like to be in it too."

Actually, Adam Joshua did.

He gave Heidi a quarter.

"Nelson, please," he said.

"It's about time," Nelson said, when Heidi threw him in jail. "I've been waiting to get arrested all day."

"That's what I thought," said Mr. D., as Heidi pushed him in with Adam Joshua and Nelson. "But you get a little tired of it after a while," he sighed. He untied a lot of rope from around his arms and chest and handed it back out to Heidi.

"It's not *being* in jail that's so bad," Mr. D. told Adam Joshua and Nelson. "It's getting arrested that takes it out of you."

As soon as they were out of jail, Adam Joshua took Nelson to see the fortune-teller. He made him wash his hands first.

"Well, what do you know," Gypsy Jade said, looking at Nelson's palm. "Cleanest all day. Let's see," she said, studying the lines. "You're going to be rich and famous, and tall, dark, and handsome, and you'll always have your dog."

"No dog," Nelson told her. "Fish."

"Them too," said Gypsy Jade.

Martha and her posse went by with Mr. D. wrapped up in a lot of rope and handcuffs.

"You could at least bring me a harmonica," he complained as they threw him in jail.

Sidney stood there looking thoughtful, and then he left the gym and came back a few minutes later with a guitar. He paid Martha a quarter to put him in jail, and he settled down beside Mr. D. and handed him the guitar.

"You play and I'll sing the 'Jailhouse Blues,'" Sidney said.

"This fling's in full swing!" Mrs. Rodriguez said, galloping past.

One of the biggest crowds was at the Dunk Tank.

A fourth-grade teacher, Miss Willow, was sitting out on a platform over a tank of water. All the fourth graders were lining up and paying to throw balls at the lever that would dump her into the tank.

Almost everybody missed, but one boy hit the lever right on target, and Miss Willow got a terrible look on her face and slid off the platform into the water.

Everybody cheered and applauded. Miss Willow came up dripping wet, trying to smile.

"Somebody's going to pay for this with extra homework," she joked.

Everybody laughed except the boy who dunked her, and he started looking really worried.

A buzzer went off and Miss Willow climbed out of the tank, and Ms. D. went to take her place on the platform.

All of Adam Joshua's class lined up to buy balls to dunk her.

"This is going to be great!" said Jonesy.

"It's going to be terrific!" said Sidney.

Nobody could do it.

"Maybe if somebody else goes first," Angie said, leaving her place at the front of the line.

Nobody was about to go first.

"I don't think she'd get mad," Heidi said. "But if I dunked her, I'd feel just awful."

"Well, I wouldn't," said Elliot, crowding in at the front of the line and winding up his pitching arm.

Elliot threw all of his balls, and then he grabbed all of Sidney's, and all of Philip's.

Everybody held their breath. Elliot missed every time.

"Thank goodness!" said Ms. D.

Mr. D. got out of jail and escaped the next posse, and came up with an armload of balls.

"Well, hi there," he said, smiling innocently at Ms. D.

Ms. D. groaned and closed her eyes.

Mr. D. threw three balls, and then he bought three more, and he bought three after that. He missed every time.

"Thank goodness, thank goodness, thank goodness!" said Ms. D.

"Excuse me," Mr. D. called out to Ms. D., "I'm a little short on money. Is your purse close by?"

"Fat chance," said Ms. D.

"I'll lend you more money," said Elliot. He went over and bought six balls and brought them to Mr. D.

"Why, Elliot," said Mr. D. "You're a gentleman."

"Elliot," growled Angie, "you're a rat."

Everybody held their breaths, but Mr. D. was such a terrible shot, they didn't get too worried.

The buzzer went off.

"Your turn," Ms. D. told Mr. D. as she climbed off the platform.

Mr. D. looked puzzled.

"I didn't know I had a turn," he said.

"Yep," Ms. D. said, smiling. "I told them you'd love to take a turn to raise money for the school. I told them you couldn't wait."

Mr. D. started looking worried.

Everybody helped Mr. D. climb up on the platform, and then everybody lined up.

"But you can go first," Angie said, making room for Ms. D.

Ms. D. hit the target with her first ball, and Mr. D. let out a yelp and slid into the water.

Angie hit the target and dunked Mr. D., and so did Jonesy, and Heidi, and Sidney.

The line to dunk Mr. D. got longer and longer.

"Why is that?" Mr. D. complained, dripping and shivering.

"Because Ms. D. is around the corner, pay-

ing us," said Angie, getting back into line again. "She's giving everyone a quarter to buy the balls, and if we hit the target, we get a dime besides."

"Never marry a devious woman," Mr. D. said with a sniffle.

———

Finally Mr. D. got to climb down, and everyone helped dry him off.

"I just heard," Ms. D. came over to tell them. "So far, our jail has made more money than anything else here! The Dunk Tank is coming in second."

Everybody cheered and jumped around and congratulated themselves.

"You're welcome," sneezed Mr. D.

———

The fling was winding down.

Adam Joshua dug deep in his pockets, and came out with all the money he'd been saving. There was a lot of it. He put every bit into the jail box.

"Elliot, please," he told Sheriff Nate.

"Well, why didn't you say so?" Nelson asked. He dug in his pockets and came up with the rest of his money. He put it in the jail box too.

"Double Elliot," he told Nate.

A lot of people lined up to put money in the box.

"Elliot," said Sidney.

"Elliot," said Heidi.

"Absolutely Elliot," said Angie.

"Hold on a minute," Ms. D. said, coming over. "We can't keep someone in jail for that long!"

"That's okay," said Angie. "You can let him out sooner. We just all wanted to feel like we helped put him there."

A lot of people pounced on Elliot and dragged him off to jail.

"I want my lawyer!" Elliot yelled.

"It's a good thing we didn't add the tunnel," said Jonesy.

———

Adam Joshua and Nelson decided to leave while Elliot was still locked up.

"That way I can pretend that he's in there all weekend," said Adam Joshua.

On their way to get Nelson's fish, they passed the raffle table.

The only things left were Sebastian and Bruno.

Ralph and Jonesy were trading.

"I'd rather have a quiet lizard than that bird," Jonesy said. "A lizard can't nag."

"I'd rather have something with personality any day," said Ralph.

They shook hands on it.

"Shape up, Mister!" said Sebastian.

"Of course, we can always change our minds, can't we?" Ralph asked, looking worried.

————

"I may sue!" Elliot yelled as they left the gym.

George was sitting, waiting for Adam Joshua, right outside the school door. He had the flowered hat in his teeth.

Adam Joshua wasn't a bit surprised.

He put the hat on George and told him the best joke he'd ever told.

It had three elephants, two dogs, and a monkey in it.

George howled.

"Adam Joshua," said Nelson, howling with

laughter himself, "that's the funniest joke I've ever heard. Why didn't you put it in the show?"

George was still chuckling.

"I saved it especially for George," said Adam Joshua.

Not many people would have understood that.

"That's great, Adam Joshua," said Nelson. "And my boss fish, Julius, is just going to flip when he sees these." He patted his bags of new goldfish happily.

George stopped laughing when he noticed the fish.

"I know," Adam Joshua sighed, sitting on George while Nelson got a good head start.

Then he let George lead the way home.